CONTENTS

GRAB THESE!

Are you ready to create some amazing pictures? Wait a minute! Before you begin drawing, you will need a few important pieces of equipment.

PENS AND PENCILS

You can use a variety of drawing tools including pens, chalks, pencils and paints. But to begin with, use an ordinary HB pencil.

PAPER

Use a clean sheet of paper for your final drawings. Scrap paper is useful and cheap for your practice work.

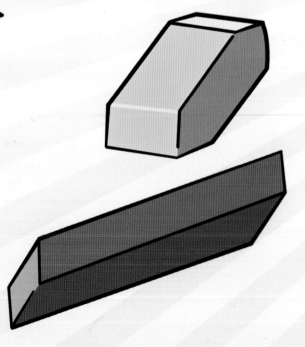

ERASERS

Everyone makes mistakes! That's why every artist has a good eraser. When you rub out a mistake, do it gently. Scrubbing hard at your paper will ruin your drawing and possibly even rip it.

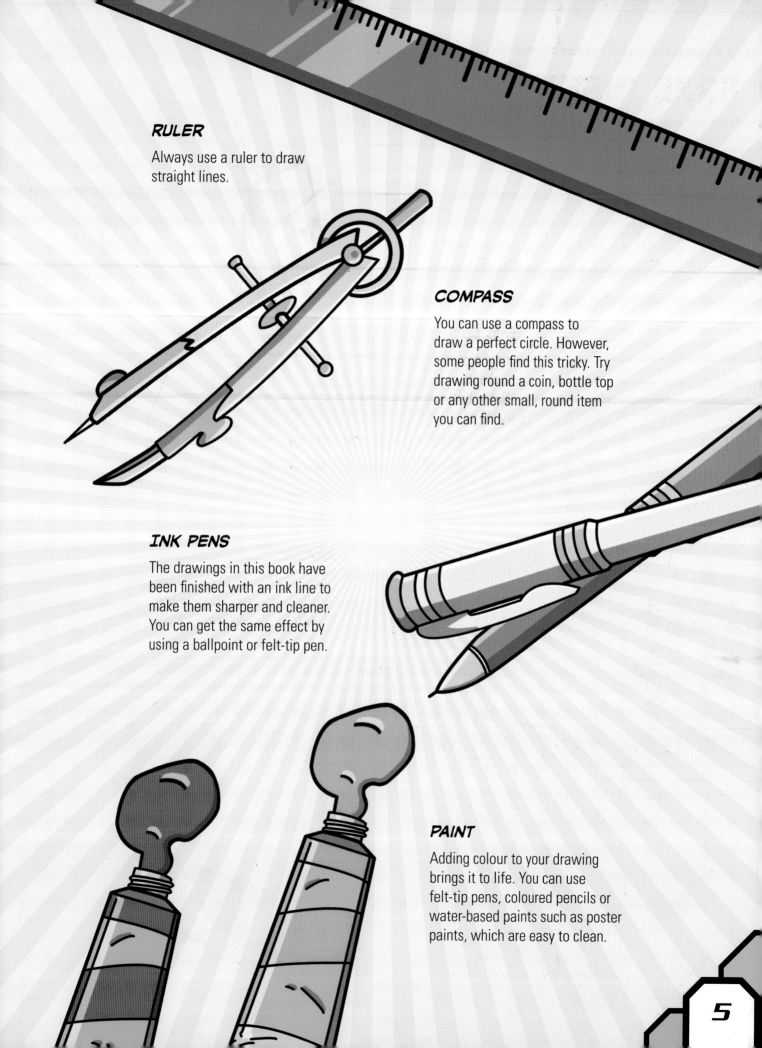

RULER

Always use a ruler to draw straight lines.

COMPASS

You can use a compass to draw a perfect circle. However, some people find this tricky. Try drawing round a coin, bottle top or any other small, round item you can find.

INK PENS

The drawings in this book have been finished with an ink line to make them sharper and cleaner. You can get the same effect by using a ballpoint or felt-tip pen.

PAINT

Adding colour to your drawing brings it to life. You can use felt-tip pens, coloured pencils or water-based paints such as poster paints, which are easy to clean.

GETTING STARTED

In this book we use a simple two-colour system to show you how to draw a picture. Just remember: new lines are blue lines!

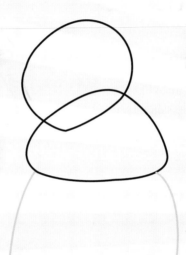

ADDING MORE DETAIL

As you move on to the next step, the lines you have already drawn will be shown in black. The new lines for that stage will appear in blue.

STARTING WITH STEP 1

The first lines you will draw are very simple shapes. They will be shown in blue, like this. You should draw them with a normal HB pencil.

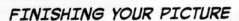

FINISHING YOUR PICTURE

When you reach the final stage you will see the image in full colour with a black ink line. Inking a picture means tracing the main lines with a black pen. After the ink dries, use your eraser to remove all the pencil lines before adding your colour.

You can make your drawings more exciting by adding special effects. It will also make your stories more fun if your characters have special powers. Here are some basic effects you can use on your creations:

LIGHTNING BLAST

Give your characters lightning powers! Add blue-coloured jagged lines coming from their hands or weapons. This will make it look like they are shooting lightning bolts.

SPARKLE-RIFFIC

Why not give some characters magical powers? Add sparkles of different-sized stars around their hands, like this.

HEATING IT UP

Give your characters fire power by adding flames. Flames are rounded at the bottom but shaped like wavy spikes at the top. Colour the centre of the flames in a light yellow.

VILLAIN

There's no doubt that this guy is a villain. His pale, sneering face and red robotic eye make him look really scary!

STEP 1

Start by drawing the shape of your villain's long body and legs. Add a head with a pointy chin.

STEP 2

Then draw two straight lines to make his legs and waist.

STEP 3

Next, draw his arms and feet. Add two ears and two lines for his nose. Join the head to the body with a neck. Draw two short lines for the collar of his jacket.

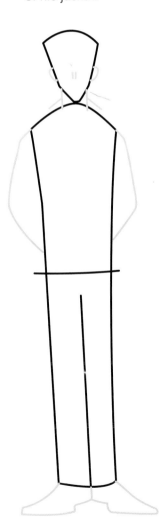

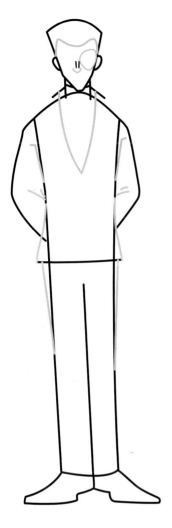

STEP 6

Colour him in using shades such as purple, red, black and blue. Use shading around the edges so that he looks 3-D.

STEP 4

Add long, curved lines to make the shape and folds of his suit. Don't forget his hairline and that scary robotic eye.

STEP 5

Now you can add the crazy hair, shirt, tie and suit outlines. Add the rest of the robotic eye and a small mouth. Finally, finish his trousers.

SUPER TIP!

You can make your villain look even more scary by giving him incredible mind powers.

- Draw a scribbly semi-circle around his head. Then add long, wavy lines, spreading outwards.

GIRL GENIUS

With her big glasses and white lab coat, Girl Genius looks super brainy. She is always thinking up new inventions to save the world from danger.

STEP 1

First, draw the girl's white lab coat and her head.

STEP 2

Next, draw two sausage shapes for the tops of her arms.

STEP 3

Add forearms, wide trousers and the outline of her hair.

STEP 4

Draw her face and neck. Add hands, feet, and the opening of her lab coat.

STEP 5

Add her glasses, the two flasks and the details on her face and coat.

STEP 6

Finally, colour her in. Leave her jacket white so that it looks like a scientist's lab coat.

FIRE SPIRIT

The **Fire Spirit** is an evil creature with magical powers. He has a long face, pointy ears and a nasty grin. He wants to set the whole world on fire!

STEP 1

First, draw a tall shape like this for the spirit's robe.

STEP 2

Add his pointy head and the wide sleeves of his robe.

STEP 3

Draw those long, pointy ears, his neck, claw-like fingers, and flames of fire around his feet.

STEP 4

Now draw the flames shooting out of his hands and around his feet. The flames should curl upwards.

STEP 5

Draw his evil eyes, tiny nose and sneaky smile. Give his eyes tiny black pupils to make him look really wicked. Then add lines to suggest the folds in his long, flowing robe.

STEP 6

Colour your villain with spooky purple, hot red and yellow.

SUPER TIP!

- When colouring in flames, start with a yellow colour in the middle parts of the flame.

- Add red and orange colours as you move towards the outside of your flames.

ANCIENT WARRIOR

This tough old warrior is armed only with a simple wooden staff. His face is hidden beneath a wide-brimmed straw hat.

STEP 1

First, draw the warrior's bean-shaped body and the lower part of his jacket. Don't forget the wide fan shape for his hat.

STEP 2

Add his curved legs.

STEP 3

Next draw his chin, feet and wide sleeves.

STEP 4

Sketch in his hair, beard, nose and mouth. Draw his hands and curve his fingers as if they are gripping something. Draw lines to make the tops of his slippers and his belt.

STEP 5

Draw a staff in his clenched hands, and add detail to his wide hat.

STEP 6

Colour your ancient warrior. Shade his face and shoulder to show the shadow cast by his hat.

MARTIAL ARTIST

This martial artist is crouching low to the ground, ready to attack. His special pose and determined face tell us he's a skilled fighter.

STEP 1

First, draw a peanut shape for his body and a pot shape for his hips. Add a small circle for his head.

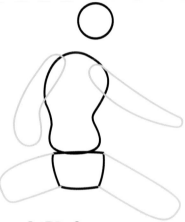

STEP 2

Add sausage shapes for his arms and thighs.

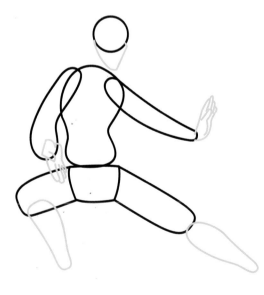

STEP 3

Draw a pointed chin, graceful hands and flowing lower legs.

STEP 4

Carefully draw feet, cuffs and hair.

STEP 5

Add his narrow eyes, nose and serious mouth. Then draw the final details of his clothing.

SUPER TIP!

The strapping on this martial artist's leg is easy to draw. Just follow these steps:

- First draw your straps as simple crosses down his leg.

- Add lines on either side.

- Erase the cross you started with and colour in the straps.

STEP 6

Colour your character. Use shading to make him stand out from the page.

MINI MONSTER

This big-eyed mini monster looks cute. He has huge ears and long whiskers. Does he fight other mini monsters in an arena, or is he a pet? You decide!

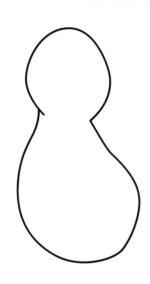

STEP 1

Firstly, draw a shape like a wobbly peanut.

STEP 2

Draw two large leaf-shaped ears, a curve for a nose, and two club-like arms.

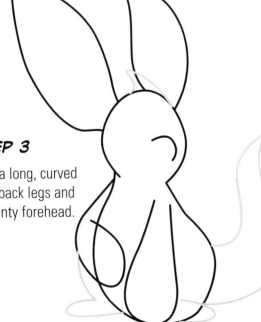

STEP 3

Add a long, curved tail, back legs and a pointy forehead.

STEP 4

Now it's time to draw his big eyes, small mouth, and claws. Sketch in details for the ear on the left and the back paws.

STEP 5

Add long whiskers. Then cover your mini monster's body in spots… or stripes if you prefer.

STEP 6

Now colour your mini monster in any shade you like. When it comes to monsters, there are no rules. Anything goes!

MAGICAL GIRL

This fun-loving magical girl looks like she's about to leap off the page. She has big, cute manga eyes and bright blue hair!

STEP 1

Start by drawing the girl's body and head.

STEP 2

Add sausage-shaped upper arms and a wide skirt.

STEP 3

Draw ears and a mouth. Now join her head to her body with a neck. Add forearms, thighs and a band around her waist.

STEP 4

Add her hair, hands and lower legs. Don't forget the collar and the bow that's behind her waist.

STEP 5

Sketch her sleeves, tie and feet before adding those amazing eyes.

STEP 6

Now you are ready to add some colour. Bright and bold looks best.

SUPER TIP!

- **Big, cute manga eyes are easy to draw if you build them up from simple round shapes:**

- Draw two ovals for the main outlines of the eyes.

- Add nice large irises in the centre.

- Use two curves to make the tops of the eye shapes. Add lines at the bottom for the lower eyelids.

- Draw a couple of eyebrows and you have your big manga eyes!

SAMURAI

Samurai were brave Japanese warriors. This one is tall and proud with a square jaw. He wears a green robe and carries a long samurai sword.

  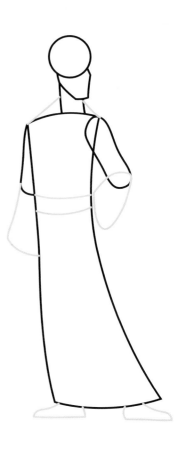

STEP 1

First, draw a long, curved rectangle shape for the samurai's robe. Add a small circle for his head.

STEP 2

Draw a square jaw and two lines for his neck. Then draw sausage shapes for his arms.

STEP 3

Next, add his shoulders and the gaping sleeves of his robe. Draw a belt and his feet.

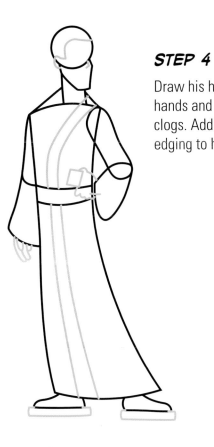

STEP 4

Draw his hairline, hands and wooden clogs. Add the edging to his robe.

STEP 5

Draw his face, long sword, and topknot. Finish off the wooden clogs.

STEP 6

Finally, colour in your samurai. A strong green colour makes his robe stand out.

23

LITTLE OLD LADY

This lady is so happy. Her round body makes her look very cuddly and kind. Her wide open mouth and closed eyes show that she's really laughing.

STEP 1

Draw a mushroom shape for her upper body and a pebble shape for her head.

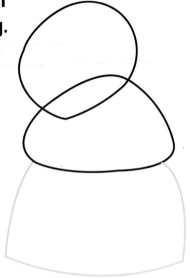

STEP 2

Draw a thick shape for her lower body.

STEP 3

Add her hairline and mouth. Then draw the wide sleeves of her robe.

STEP 4

Carefully draw her hands, hair, tiny nose and belt.

STEP 5

Add the final details, including curves for her eyes and the bowl of noodles.

STEP 6

Colour the little old lady in nice, soft colours.

CAT GIRL

This girl has a cat's furry tail, big ears and long whiskers. She's very playful and loves playing tricks on people!

STEP 1

First, draw an oval for her head, and this curved, pointy shape for her body.

STEP 2

Draw two sausage shapes for her legs and long arms.

STEP 3

Add her cat-like ears and the rest of her legs.

STEP 4

Her 'S'-shaped tail comes next. Then add her neck, the details of her clothing, her hands, feet and face. Don't forget those big manga eyes!

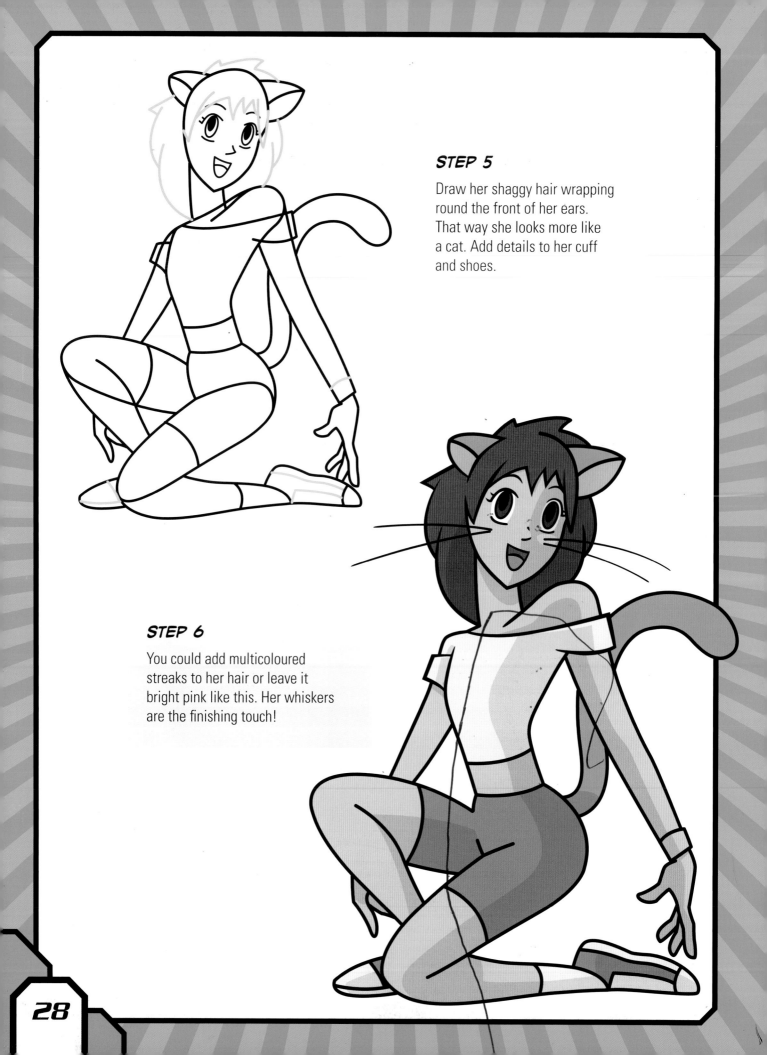

STEP 5

Draw her shaggy hair wrapping round the front of her ears. That way she looks more like a cat. Add details to her cuff and shoes.

STEP 6

You could add multicoloured streaks to her hair or leave it bright pink like this. Her whiskers are the finishing touch!

Sumo wrestlers are very large and heavy. This one squats down low as he faces his opponent. During fights, a sumo wears a silk loincloth called a 'mawashi'.

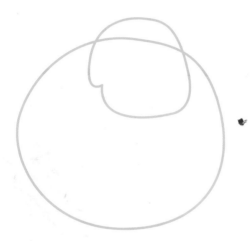

STEP 1

Sumos are large, so start the body and head with these big, round shapes.

STEP 2

Add the very rounded arms and legs, and his mawashi.

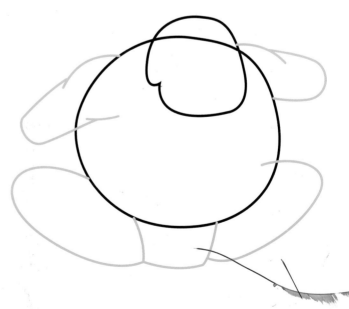

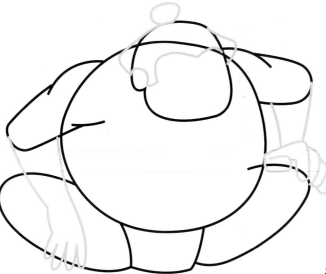

STEP 3

Add the rest of his arms and hands. Then draw the sumo's hairstyle.

STEP 4

Add details to his chest. Finish off the legs and feet.

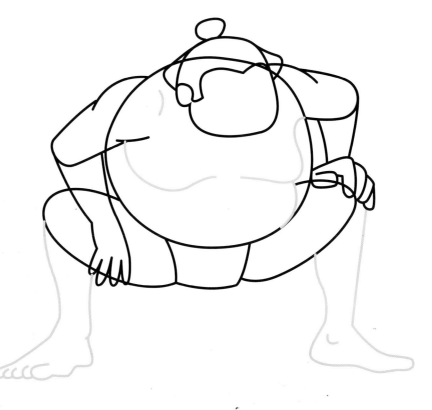

STEP 5

Draw his face and hair. He has heavy eyebrows, a wide mouth and a fierce expression. Add the pieces hanging down from his mawashi. They are called 'sagari'.

STEP 6

Sumo wrestlers believe the colour of their mawashi affects their luck in matches. Red must be this sumo's lucky colour!

GLOSSARY

3-D Three-dimensional. A 3-D object has height, width and depth.

arena An enclosed area, often circular or oval-shaped, for performances.

clog A wooden shoe.

cuff The end of a sleeve, around the wrist.

HB A pencil that is neither soft not hard, but something in between.

iris The coloured central part of the eye.

loincloth A piece of cloth that wraps around the hips.

mawashi A sumo wrestler's loincloth.

pupil The black circle in the centre of the eye, which controls the amount of light entering the eye.

staff A long stick used as a support for walking or as a weapon.

FURTHER READING

How to Draw Manga by David Antram (Book House, 2010)

Kids Draw Big Book of Everything Manga by Chris Hart (Watson-Guptill, 2009)

Mastering Manga with Mark Crilley by Mark Crilley (Impact Books, 2012)

WEBSITES

www.drawingnow.com/how-to-draw-manga.html

www.howtodrawmanga.com

www.wikihow.com/Draw-Manga

INDEX